KT-504-415

*Also by Jill Murphy
and published by Macmillan*

Whatever Next!
On the Way Home

This book
belongs to

First published 1980 by Macmillan Children's Books.

This revised edition published 1995
by Macmillan Children's Books
a division of Macmillan Publishers Limited
20 New Wharf Road
London N1 9RR
Basingstoke and Oxford
Associated companies throughout the world
www.panmacmillan.com

ISBN 978-0-333-63198-0

Copyright © Jill Murphy 1980

All rights reserved. No part of this publication may be
reproduced or transmitted in any form,
or by any means, without permission.

26

A CIP catalogue record for this book is available
from the British Library.

Printed in China

PEACE AT LAST

JILL MURPHY

MACMILLAN
CHILDREN'S BOOKS

For Graham
and Caroline
and their
children.

The hour was late.

Mr. Bear was tired
Mrs. Bear was tired
and
Baby Bear was tired. . .

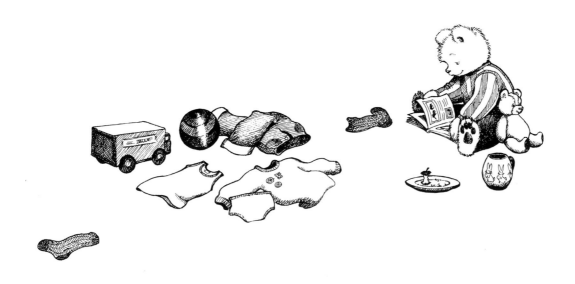

. . .so they all went to bed.

Mrs. Bear fell asleep.

Mr. Bear didn't.

Mrs. Bear began to snore.
"SNORE," went Mrs. Bear,
"SNORE, SNORE, SNORE."
"Oh NO!" said Mr. Bear,
"I can't stand THIS."
So he got up and went to
sleep in Baby Bear's room.

Baby Bear was not asleep either.
He was lying in bed pretending
to be an aeroplane.
"NYAAOW!" went Baby Bear,
"NYAAOW! NYAAOW!"
"Oh NO!" said Mr. Bear,
"I can't stand THIS."
So he got up
and went to sleep in the living-room.

TICK-TOCK . . . went the living-room
clock. . . .TICK-TOCK, TICK-TOCK.
CUCKOO! CUCKOO!
"Oh NO!" said Mr. Bear,
"I can't stand THIS."
So he went off to sleep in the kitchen.

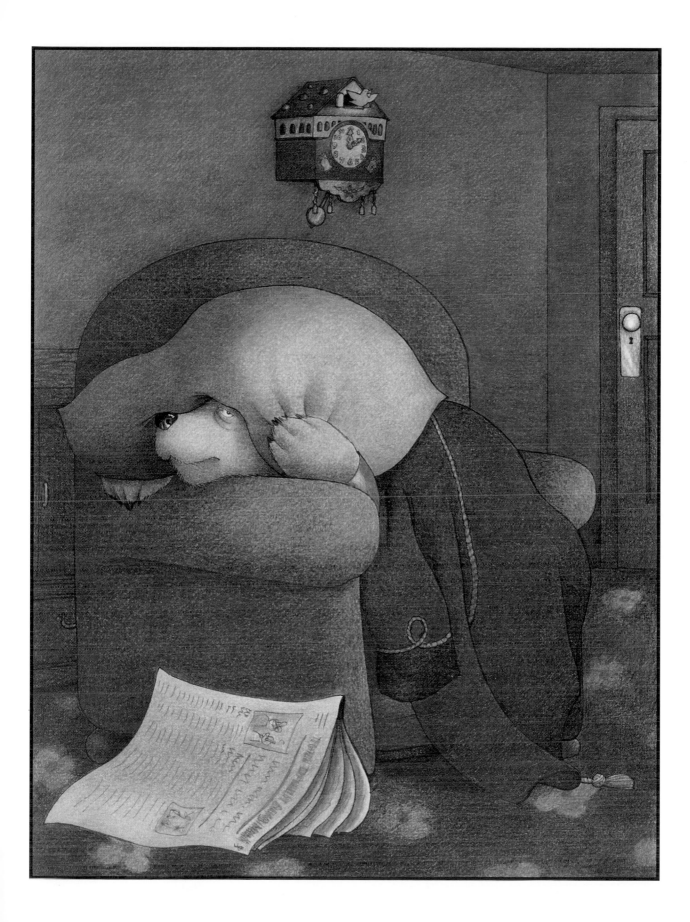

DRIP, DRIP . . . went the leaky
kitchen tap.
HMMMMMMMMMMM . . .
went the refrigerator.
"Oh NO," said Mr. Bear,
"I can't stand THIS."
So he got up
and went to sleep in the garden.

Well, you would not believe
what noises there are in
the garden at night.
"TOO-WHIT-TOO-WHOO!"
went the owl.
"SNUFFLE, SNUFFLE," went
the hedgehog.
"MIAAAOW!" sang the cats
on the wall.
"Oh, NO!" said Mr. Bear,
"I can't stand THIS."
So he went off to sleep in
the car.

It was cold in the car
and uncomfortable, but
Mr. Bear was so tired
that he didn't notice.
He was just falling asleep
when all the birds started to
sing and the sun peeped in at
the window.
"TWEET TWEET!" went the birds.
SHINE, SHINE . . . went the sun.
"Oh NO!" said Mr. Bear,
"I can't stand THIS."
So he got up and went back
into the house.

In the house, Baby Bear was
fast asleep, and Mrs. Bear had
turned over and wasn't snoring
any more.
Mr. Bear got into bed and closed his
eyes.
"Peace at last," he said to himself.

BRRRRRRRRRRRRRR! went the
alarm-clock, BRRRRRR!
Mrs. Bear sat up and rubbed her eyes.
"Good morning, dear," she said.
"Did you sleep well?"
"Not VERY well, dear," yawned
Mr. Bear.
"Never mind," said Mrs. Bear. "I'll
bring you a nice cup of tea."

And she did.